Mary
Was a Little Lamb

Gloria Rand
Illustrated by Ted Rand

Henry Holt and Company • New York

Henry Holt and Company, LLC
Publishers since 1866
115 West 18th Street
New York, New York 10011
www.henryholt.com

Library of Congress Cataloging-in-Publication Data
Rand, Gloria.
Mary was a little lamb / Gloria Rand; illustrated by Ted Rand.
Summary: Mrs. Paradise figures out what to do with Mary, a wayward,
abandoned lamb. Based on a true story.
1. Sheep—Juvenile fiction. [1. Sheep—Fiction. 2. Orphaned animals—Fiction.]
I. Rand, Ted, ill. II. Title.
PZ10.3.R167Mar 2004   [E]—dc21   2003007066

ISBN 0-8050-6816-3
First Edition—2004
Printed in the United States of America on acid-free paper. ∞

10 9 8 7 6 5 4 3 2 1

To Alice Seed, a dear and book-wise friend
— G. R. and T. R.

Mary was a little lamb. She was one of a
set of twins born on an abandoned farm on
Cranberry Island.

When she was only
a few hours old, her mother
wandered off with the other twin. Mary's
mother had forgotten she had two little lambs,
not just one.

Mary was left all alone in the middle of a big
field. "Baa," she cried. "Baa, baa."

Along came Mrs. Paradise, bumping across the field on her
bicycle. "Well, who do we have here?" She brought her bicycle to
a squeaky stop. "Let me guess. Is your name Mary?"

"Baa," Mary answered, and tottered over to Mrs. Paradise.

Mrs. Paradise gently picked up the little lamb. "Would you like to come live at my house?"

She tucked Mary under her arm and pedaled off toward her beach cottage, steering with only one hand.

Mrs. Paradise put Mary in a dry, cozy garden shed. "You'll live here until you're bigger and stronger," she explained as she fed the lamb a bottle of warm milk. "Then you can live in my backyard."

Mary grew quickly. Soon she was big enough and strong enough to live outside, where she grazed on tender green grass.

She loved to explore. One day she poked around until she discovered a hole in Mrs. Paradise's garden fence. She promptly wiggled through it.

Mary visited the neighbors' houses. She played with the children and chased around with their dogs, just as if she were a dog herself.

When the island's tiny commuter boat tooted its whistle to say
it was about to dock, Mary trotted down to greet the passengers.
"Baa, Mary, baa," they called as they came ashore.
"Baa," Mary answered. "Baa, baa."

Soon Mary knew everyone on the island.
She was friends with all the children and
followed them everywhere.

"That lamb of yours is marking up the school porch with her sharp little hooves," complained the maintenance man for the island's one-room schoolhouse.

It was raining when they reached the abandoned farm. Sheep were crowded on the porch and inside the dilapidated old farmhouse, trying to stay dry.

"Come and meet your family, Mary," Mrs. Paradise said.

Mary stayed right where she was.
She showed no interest in her flock,
and when Mrs. Paradise finally headed
back home, Mary followed.

"What am I going to do about this dear little lamb?" Mrs. Paradise wondered. Then she remembered the zoo across the bay. Maybe someone there could help.

Mrs. Paradise called the zoo and told the keeper about Mary.
"Sounds like she might be happy in our petting zoo," the keeper
said. "We'd be glad to have her come here to live."

The next morning Mrs. Paradise took
Mary aboard the commuter boat. They
stood together on the deck and rode
across to the mainland, where a truck
was waiting to take Mary to the zoo.

"Baa, baa," Mary cried as she was loaded into the truck.

Mrs. Paradise waved to her. "Baa, Mary, baa. I'm going to miss you terribly."

The whole island missed the little lamb. When Mrs. Paradise went to visit Mary the next week, she was startled to find the boat full. The teacher, the maintenance man, and all the students were already aboard.

"We want to see Mary too," they explained.

At the zoo, Mrs. Paradise led the way to the petting pens.

"There she is!" Everyone pointed and smiled at Mary, who was surrounded by young admirers.

"Baa, Mary, baa!" Mrs. Paradise hurried over and gave the lamb a big hug.

"Baa, baa," Mary bleated, looking pleased with herself.

"Do you know her?" the children from the mainland asked. "She's our favorite."

"Yes, we all know Mary," Mrs. Paradise and the islanders answered. "She's our favorite too."

✦ Author's Note ✦

Some years ago the elderly owner of a small farm on Decatur Island in Washington State died. His sheep were left to fend for themselves, eating grass wherever they could find it. Uncared for, their thick wool coats became matted, full of burrs and dirt. Soon the whole flock looked terrible.

Island residents decided something had to be done about these neglected animals. They adopted the sheep as a community project. Two sheepherders came to round up the sheep and shear their woolly coats. A farm veterinarian visited also, to give the sheep shots to protect them from disease. It was decided to limit the flock to eighty sheep. Extra lambs were sold at auction in the fall. The money from these sales, and from the sale of the sheared wool, was used to care for the flock, which was allowed to remain free. The sheep shearing became a much-anticipated annual event in the summer, with a huge picnic, games, storytelling, and music.

This story is based on a little lamb from that flock. She was found and raised by the Dunlap family, who named her Mary. She grew up playing with island children and their dogs. She refused to have anything to do with the island flock. Mary became a real pest. She'd baa to be let into houses at night, and she ate schoolwork out of notebooks that were left unattended. If anyone was carrying a grocery bag, she was right there, trying to reach in and pull out her favorite snack, a Mars bar. The real Mary now lives at the Woodland Park Petting Zoo in Seattle, where she enjoys the attention of her many admiring visitors.